UPENDO HUSHINDA YOTE

BY: R. D. Solomon Jr.

Upendo Hushinda Yote

By: R. D. Solomon Jr.

TABLE OF CONTENTS

CHAPTER ONE: KATIKA MWANZO (IN THE BEGINNING)

Long ago, in the land of Alkebulan, there were two great tribes. They were named the Mansa Kemets, known for their strong leadership and heritage, and the Ase Awo, known for their spiritual power and wisdom. Among the Mansa Kemets, lived a little boy named Bakari. Among the Ase Awo, was a little girl named Jameela. Though they were from different tribes, Bakari and Jameela loved to play together in the open fields, wrestling and practicing their hunting skills. They both loved competition, so much that almost everything they did became one.

"I bet I'll put a dent in that tree before you with my slingshot," Bakari said. "Yea? We will see about that. You may be able to shoot farther, but I have always had better aim than you." Jameela replied. Bakari squinted his eyes before walking towards Jameela to shoulder nudge her. "Tell you what put your money where your mouth is. If you win, I will give you my tribe necklace. If I win, I get yours" Bakari said. Jameela looked down at her necklace, grabbed it, and hesitated. "Fine, I think your tribe's symbol will look good around my neck," Jameela said.

As Bakari drew the line in the dirt, Jameela stepped to the line. After loading her slingshot with a smooth stone, she pulled back as far as possible, closed one eye, and released. The stone hit the tree right in the center, leaving a large dent. "I win!"

Jameela exclaimed. “You haven’t won yet. I still have my turn.” Bakari replied. “Nope, you said whoever puts a dent in the tree first, so I win,” Jameela responded. “But I didn’t get a chance to go,” Bakari replied. “Tough, now hand it over. You lost fair and square.” Jameela said.

“No!” Bakari exclaimed. “I said hand it over!” Jameela exclaimed. Jameela reached for the necklace around Bakari’s neck. Bakari pushed her away. Jameela tackled Bakari to the ground to retrieve the necklace. As they fell she accidentally scratched him on his left cheek. This angered Bakari, so he retaliated by pushing her off him. At the same time, her right hand ripped the necklace from his neck. As Jameela fell back, her right arm fell on a rock fracturing it. Jameela immediately screamed in pain that could be heard by both tribes in the distance. Bakari stood up and immediately apologized nervously for what he had done. “I’m, I'm, sorry,” Bakari uttered.

Bakari ran back to his village, leaving Jameela to tend to her wounds, and for her tribe to find her.

CHAPTER TWO: KUTENGANA (SEPARATION)

Jameela's father, Jabali, who was also the leader of the Ase Awo, came running as fast as he could to Jameela's rescue. Upon arriving in the open field, his concern is portrayed first, then his anger. "What happened Jameela? Who did this to you?" Jameela looked up and saw the look on Jabali's face. She didn't want to get Bakari in trouble so she said, "I slipped and fell on a rock while I was playing." Jabali paused, looked around, and took a deep breath. "Come on baby girl, let's get you home," Jabali said. Jabali picked Jameela up from the ground and carried her back to the village to be tended to by the village doctor. She kept Bakari's necklace in her pouch until she was safe in her room. Once, tucked away for the night, she pulled it out, looked at it for a while, put it back in her pouch, and fell asleep.

On the other side of the land, Bakari ran home as fast as he could. As he was running, he had forgotten he had a scratch on his face that he had to explain. As Bakari entered his home, he tried to go straight to his room, only to be called back by his mother, Bititi, the leader of the Mansa Kemets.

"Bakari! Come!" Bititi said. "Yes, mama?" Bakari answered. "What did I tell you about leaving and not letting me know where you are going? These are dangerous times. Anything can happen to you. I do not want to have this conversation again." Bititi said. "Yes, mama," Bakari said. What happened to your face? Come here." Bititi told Bakari.

“ I scratched it while climbing a tree,” Bakari said.

“Boy, what am I going to do with you? Go wash up so I can clean that scar. Dinner will be ready soon.” Bititi said. After dinner, Bakari sat in his room. Bititi came into Bakari’s room as he was lying down and asked, “Bakari, where is your necklace? I noticed you weren’t wearing it?” Bakari’s eyes widened and he was as nervous as ever. I lost it in the fields. I’m sorry mama. Bititi’s eyes squinted as she said, “You will find that necklace tomorrow. It is a significant part of who we are. Do you understand? “Yes, mama,” Bakari said. Bititi kissed Bakari’s forehead and said, “Very well, goodnight son. I love you”

CHAPTER THREE: UTUME WA ROHO

(GHOST MISSION)

The next morning, Bakari woke up early and nervous. He knew if he came back empty-handed, his mother would be furious. Yet, he had to at least make it look like he attempted to find the necklace, though he knew where it was and could not retrieve it. So, after washing his face, he left to make up a plan.

"What am I going to do?" Bakari said to himself. "I can't go back to my mother without my necklace. It's our tribe's symbol. It is everything we stand for. It's everything we are, everything we will be." Bakari looked up at the sky and marveled at the clouds. He was mesmerized by the shapes of the clouds. They looked like warriors, horses, and chariots in war. He often dreamed of one day having his own army and being the leader of the tribe when it was his time.

After daydreaming of the future, Bakari found himself back at the tree in the open field. He sat and he rested a bit to try to configure a plan. He looked left, then looked right. Then, he looked left again. "Why did you leave me!?!" Jameela exclaimed. Bakari stood as if he had seen a ghost. He stood up, looked Jameela up and down, and backed away slowly. "Answer me!" Jameela exclaimed. This angered Bakari. "Give me my necklace back!" Bakari exclaimed.

"Not til' you answer my question! Jameela replied. "You know what, keep it! I hate you!" Bakari angrily shouted. Jameela's eyes filled with tears as she said, "I'm going home. You will never see that necklace again." "Fine, I don't need it anyway!" Bakari shouted as he watched Jameela walk back to her village. Yet, he was still at a loss for how he was going to get his necklace back. He was determined to not go home without it. So, he decided to follow Jameela back to her village.

CHAPTER FOUR: KUKAMATWA (CAUGHT)

Bakari was very careful to stay hidden behind trees and bushes as he followed Jameela back to her village. As they came upon the village, he had to think fast about how he was going to get into the village without being seen. It was very dangerous to try to enter a village of a tribe you did not belong to without having official business. Bakari looked around and saw merchants entering and leaving the village pulling carts with horses. That is when the idea struck him.

Bakari decided to sneak into one of the merchants' carts and ride into the village. Once inside, he waited until the cart stopped and jumped out the back. As his feet hit the ground, he immediately looked around and was amazed at the tall huts and scenery. To interrupt his amazement, a village elder asked him, “Are you lost, boy?” Bakari, scared, uttered, “My dad is the merchant. I am just waiting for him.”

The village elder squinted his eyes and said, “Very well, be careful.” Then, he slowly walked away. Bakari took a deep breath and knew his time was limited to find Jameela, retrieve his necklace, and get out of there. Bakari found space between two huts to hide in and search for Jameela from there. He soon spotted her headed to what looked to be her home. Bakari took a mental note of where it was and waited until nightfall to try to sneak in and get back what was rightfully his.

A large fire lit the center of the village as people were getting ready to rest for the evening.

Bakari avoided the fire by staying in the shadows until he got to Jameela's hut. Two small lanterns were lit, one in each room. Bakari knew he only had one shot at finding the necklace, so he had to choose which light he was going to follow. Figuring Jameela's room was in the back of the hut instead of the front, he waited until it was quiet and ran in straight to the back. To his unfortunate surprise, he was met by Jabali who was not pleased in the least to see a boy in his hut uninvited.

CHAPTER FIVE: HAKUNA KUTOROKA

(NO ESCAPE)

Bakari was frozen in place as Jabali stood and towered over him. “What are you doing here boy? Who sent you?” Jabali asked. Bakari stood shaking and silent. His words couldn’t seem to form a response. “Get out of here and don’t come back!” Jabali screamed. Bakari turned with fear and began to run. After hearing her father scream, Jameela came running and bumped into Bakari. They both fell and looked at each other as if they had seen a ghost. “I said get out of here!” Jabali screamed again. Bakari got up and ran as fast as he could to the exit of the village.

Bakari’s trouble was not over, as night had fallen and he was not home. Naturally, Bakari’s mother formed a search to find him. When he saw the multiple torches and heard them calling his name, he went running for comfort in the crowd. Multiple villagers were relieved to find him, hugged him close and rejoiced as he cried. Then, his mother, Bititi walked toward him slowly. In a calm but stern voice, she asked, "Where have you been?" "I was trying to find my necklace and lost track of time. I'm sorry." Bakari said. "It is all right son. The fault is mine. I should have sent someone with you. Right now all I care about is that you are safe. Come, let's go home." Bititi said.

Then, all of a sudden, multiple torches were coming towards the villagers. Everyone got their weapons and shields ready as the torches got closer. When they came close enough, Bakari realized that the man who ran him from the hut was at the head of this group. It was the villagers from Jameela's tribe. That is when Bakari realized that he was the leader of their tribe, just as his mother was the leader of his tribe. Jameela was on his side, peeking out at Bakari, with his necklace in her hand. She looked just as nervous as Bakari.

CHAPTER SIX: MIKUTANO ISIYOTARAJIWA (UNEXPECTED RENDEZVOUS)

"Jabali, your tribe has no business here. This land belongs to the Mansa Kemets" Bititi said. "It is Ase Awo's business anywhere when someone intrudes in our village," Jabali replied. " "I am not sure who would do such a thing, but I can assure you." Bititi was interrupted by Jabali, "It was this boy here! He ran into my hut to take from me! The nerve!" Jabali exclaimed. The Manasa Kemet warriors gathered behind Bititi and the Ase Awo warriors gathered behind Jabali. "There are many things I can tolerate Jabali, but I will not tolerate lies." I think it is time for you to leave" Bititi said calmly.

"We will leave when that boy apologizes and explains why he was in our village," Jabali replied. "He doesn't have to explain a thing to you. I will not warn you again Jabali. Take your tribe and leave at once." Bititi said sternly. Jabali looked at Bakari as Bakari looked at Jameela. Jabali then looked down at Jameela before looking at Bititi's serious face. "Don't let it happen again," Jabali said. As they turned to walk away, Jameela could not take it anymore. "Wait, father! I know why he came to our village. He was looking for this." Jameel pulled the necklace from her pouch and held it up.

Bititi was astonished as she asked, "How did you get that!?!" "We had a competition and she won it from me," Bakari said. Jameela began to walk over to hand the necklace back to Bakari and she was immediately stopped by Jabali. "Was this the same day you broke your arm?" Jabali asked. Jameela did not answer. "You broke my daughter's arm!" Jabali exclaimed. "Enough of this! Give us our necklace back now and be about your way!" Bititi exclaimed. "If you all want it back, come get it!" Jabali exclaimed. The Ase Awo tribe turned to go back to their village as the Mansa Kemets stood. Bititi, infuriated with the entire situation and its circumstances exclaimed, "Jabali, this means war!" Jabali then turned once more, looked at Bititi in the distance, and exclaimed, "As you wish!"

Yet neither tribe could afford to lose any of its people or its resources. So, instead, they chose to have no dealings with one another, and no goods were traded between the two.

CHAPTER SEVEN: WAKATI (TIME)

Seven years passed and the land was peaceful. Bakari was chastised harshly for his wrongdoing and he was not allowed to leave the village for some time. Yet, with much work and trust being rebuilt, he was allowed to start venturing out again. Though he did not have his necklace, he was still Bakari, son of Bititi, Prince of the Mansa Kemets. However, there was not a day that went by that he did not think about how Jabali treated him that night. He had never felt so humiliated and embarrassed. He wanted him to know how it felt now that he was older and much stronger.

So, Bakari decided to go back to the Ase Awo village. "Mom, I am going to go practice my hunting skills," Bakari said. "Okay son, be home before we light the village fire. While you're out, please bring back some firewood." Bititi said. "Yes, mother," Bakari replied. Bakari started his way toward the Ase Awo village. As he passed the tree where he lost his necklace to Jameela, he looked at the dent in the tree where Jameela hit it with her slingshot. He paused, took a deep breath, and continued. As he reached the entrance, two guards approached him and asked, "What is your business here?"

"I need to speak to Jabali," Bakari said. "You dare speak his name as if you are friends?" One of the guards said as both drew their spears. " I am the prince of the Mansa Kamets and I must speak to him now," Bakari replied. This fuss gained Jabali's attention as he was on his way out of the village for travel. "Do you have any idea what danger you are in coming here, boy?" Jabali said. "I am no longer a boy. I am a warrior now and I have come to retrieve what is rightfully mine." Bakari said. Jabali laughed. "As I told your mother, if you want it, come get it," Jabali said. Bakari swiftly ran past the guards and Jabali and into the village. "Stop him!" Jabali exclaimed. Bakari ran straight to the hut he remembered. Jameela was napping, even through all of the commotion.

Bakari grabbed the pouch and made his way to the back side of the huts and out of the back of the village. He grabbed his necklace from the pouch and ran as fast as he could back to his village. To his surprise, he was not being chased or followed.

CHAPTER EIGHT: VITA (WAR)

As Bakari approached the Mansa Kemet village, villagers were wondering why he was running. With no time to explain, he ran right to his mother. “Mother! Mother” I have restored our honor!” Bakari said. “What are you talking about Bakari? Why are you out of breath? Where is the firewood? Bititi asked. “Mother, look,” Bakari said as he held up the necklace. “What have you done!?!” Bititi exclaimed. “You have put all of us in danger Bakari!” “But mother,” Bakari said. No buts! We have to prepare now!” Bititi replied.

Bititi stood in the middle of the village and exclaimed, “The time for war is now! We must stay vigilant, strong, and dominant! We do not know when they will strike, but believe me, they will!”

"Mother?" Bakari said. "I have done my best to raise you boy. Why would you go and do a thing like this? Have I not been good to you? Bakari dropped his head in shame. He thought getting the necklace back would bring peace and honor to the village. Yet, it seemed to only bring chaos and shame.

Meanwhile, on the other side of the land, Jabali and the Ase Awo were preparing to attack. "We leave at dusk," Jabali told the warriors. "But sir, will they not see us coming with our torches?" One warrior asked. "We will not have our torches," Jabali replied. " I am sure their village will be lit. We will have plenty of light to attack." Jameela was devastated. Someone who she once called a friend has now not only abandoned her but has now taken from her. She too was ready for war.

As dusk began to form into the night, the Ase Awo approached the Mansa Kemet village. The village fire was lit, just as Jabali said it would be. The Mansa Kemet warriors were standing in the middle of the village surrounding Bititi and Bakari, ready for war. It would have been hard to commence a surprise attack from any angle with this defense. So Jabali decided to take a different approach.

CHAPTER NINE: UKWELI (THE TRUTH)

As Jabali and Jameela approached the village, the Ase Awo warriors followed closely behind. Bititi and Bakari met them at the entrance. "Is this what you want?" Bititi asked. "Your boy invaded our village yet again. It is not what I want, it is what he wants." Jabali replied. "I took back what was rightfully mine!" Bakari exclaimed. "Quiet!" Bititi exclaimed. "Why did you leave me?" Jameela said in a salm voice. "What?" Bakari asked. "You left me in the field like a wounded animal. Why did you leave me?" "I, I was scared," Bakari said nervously.

"After all this time, you still could not teach him courage." Jabali said "And after all this time, you still ended up with a stubborn girl by your side." Bititi said. "What is she talking about father? Jameela said. "Jabali stared at Bititi as Bititi stared back at him. Bakari recalled the night they all met in the field after he ran from the hut. Bititi called Jabali by his name and Jabali did the same to Bititi. "How do you two know each other?" Bakari asked. Bititi and Jabali both dropped their heads. "Bakari…" Bititi said. "No, how do you two know each other?" Bakari asked again.

There was a long silence as the warriors from both tribes continued to stare one another down. "Bakari, Jabali is your father." Bititi said. Bakari fell to his knees. "Father, is this true?" Jameela asked. "Yes," Jabali replied. "It is also true that Bititi is your mother," Jabali added. "Why would you do this to us!?! Jameela exclaimed. "Why are we from two different tribes!?! Why are we separated in such a way!?!" Jameela asked. "Why did you keep this from us? We could have grown up with both parents!" Bakari exclaimed.

"It is not easy to say, but my stubbornness got in the way. We were once the Yoruba tribe but I wanted things one way and your father wanted them another." Bititi said. "So, we split the tribe in two and let the villagers decide on who they wanted to follow. Jameela, I took you to raise you to be the opposite of what your mother was." Jabali told Jameela. "Bakari, I took you to raise you to be everything Jabali was not. Bititi said. "Yet, we are still just the same as what you two were walking away from," Jameela said. Bititi and Jabali looked into each other's eyes, looked back at their warriors and both exclaimed, "Simama chini!" and the warriors kneeled.

CHAPTER 10: UPATANISHO (RECONCILIATION)

"Jabali, I know that I can be a bit bullheaded, but it is only because I wanted what was best for us," Bititi said. "I understand, but you also have to know everything before we can decide on things. Plus, I am the man. I am the leader." Jabali said. "I have no issues with you being the." Bakari interrupted Bititi's response. "What about us!?! What about how this makes Jameela and I feel?" Bakari asked. "Don't you think you at least of us an apology?" Jameela asked. Bititi and Jabali looked at each other and said in unison, "We're sorry." "That's not enough for me," Bakari said. A man needs his father." Bakari said. "A woman needs her mother," Jameela said.

Bakari went to hug Jabali as Jameela went to hug Bititi. They were both apprehensive at first but embraced the hugs after a few moments. Tears began to fall from all of them. Barriers began to break within them. Generational curses were weakened. Love, unconditional love, prevented war. Everyone won. The warriors cheered as Bititi's and Jabali's hands raised and their fingers locked in unison to call a truce. The tribe of Yoruba was restored and the village was repositioned to center around the tree where Jameela left the dent with her slingshot. This is confirmation that if you allow it to, love can truly conquer all.

Love never gets lost, it is only kept. –

African Proverb

www.ingramcontent.com/pod-product-compliance
Lightning Source LLC
LaVergne TN
LVHW022032200926
848481LV00007B/2659
* 9 7 9 8 2 9 5 4 0 5 9 6 9 *